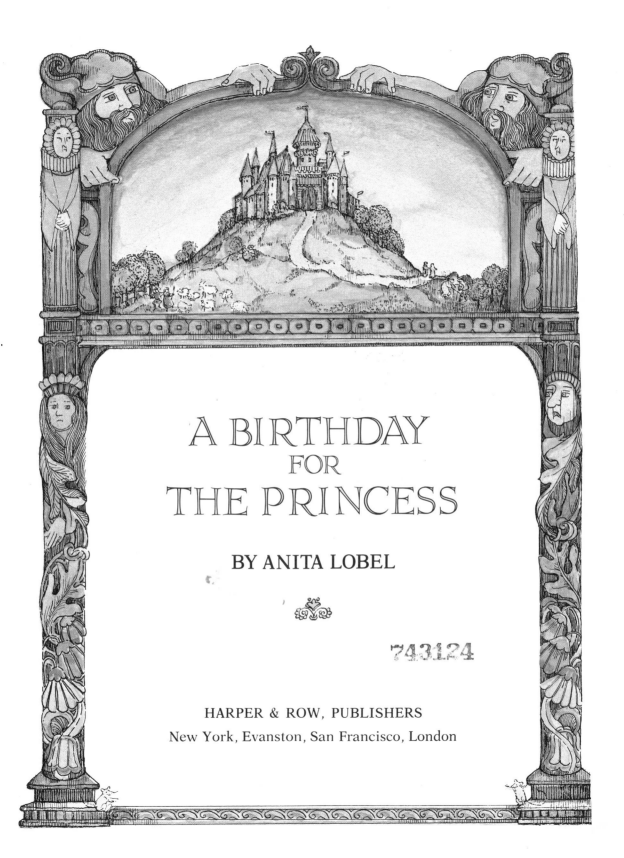

A BIRTHDAY
FOR
THE PRINCESS

BY ANITA LOBEL

HARPER & ROW, PUBLISHERS

New York, Evanston, San Francisco, London

This is for Belia

Once there was a princess who lived in a castle on top of a hill. Every morning, the princess woke up and waited for her governesses to come in and wake her.

"Wake up! Wake up, your majesty!" they said.

"I *am* awake," thought the princess.

Then the governesses washed the princess and dressed her and combed her hair.

Every morning, the king and queen came in.

"Good morning, Mother and Father," said the princess.

"Be a good princess today," said the king, "and write neatly in your copy book."

"Be a good princess today," said the queen, "and sit straight in your chair."

"Yes," said the princess.

Then the governesses taught the princess to sit straight in her chair and write neatly in her copy book.

All day the king was busy ruling the kingdom. The queen was busy ruling the palace. The princess was busy being good.

Every evening when the princess went to bed, the king and queen asked, "Was she a good princess today?"

"Yes, your majesties," answered the governesses.

"Very well, she can go to bed now," said the king and queen, and everyone went away.

"Good night," said the princess to herself, every night.

Then one morning, the governesses washed
and dressed the princess in a great hurry.

"Today is your birthday," they said. "The
king and queen are very busy planning your
grand birthday party. You sit here and be good,
and wait for the party to begin."

The princess was left alone sitting straight in
her chair. "Nobody said 'Happy birthday,'" she
thought.

Just then the princess heard music outside her window. She saw an organ-grinder, who sang and danced while his little monkey performed tricks.

"Hello, pretty girl," said the organ-grinder. "Why do you look so sad?"

"It's my birthday," said the princess.

"Happy birthday!" said the organ-grinder. "Come and dance with us."

"I can't," said the princess. "I have to be good and wait for my party to start."

Then the princess had an idea. "Come to my party," she cried. "Then we can dance!"

"Thank you. We will be there," said the organ-grinder. "See you later." He and the monkey threw kisses to the princess.

At the palace, very important guests and entertainers began to arrive. But when the organ-grinder and the monkey reached the palace gate they were stopped by the guards.

"And what are *you* doing here?" shouted one guard. "When did the king and queen invite you?"

"The princess invited us," said the organ-grinder.

"The princess does not send party invitations," snarled the other guard. "The princess sits straight in a chair and writes neatly in her copy book. Everyone knows that!"

The guards laughed, and slammed the gate in the faces of the organ-grinder and his monkey.

In the ballroom the party began. The princess received many new copy books and pens from her grandmothers, uncles, aunts, and cousins.

"The grand entertainment in honor of the princess' birthday will now begin," commanded the king.

"My friends will be here soon," thought the princess.

"The Sterling String Ensemble and The Kapusta Octet!" announced the major domo. Four violinists began to play softly, and eight large singers began to sing loudly.

"This does not sound very good," thought the princess.

"Isn't this lovely?" whispered the queen to the king.

"Wait till you hear my friends sing and play," said the princess.

"Shh! Stop mumbling while your mother is listening to music," snapped the king.

"The Noctambule Nonsense Dancers!" announced the major domo. A group of dancers began to dance. All the relatives applauded.

"My friends can dance much better than that," the princess said to herself.

"The Juvenile Juggling Team of Pergolesi, Pergolesi, and Smith!" announced the major domo. Pergolesi, Pergolesi, and Smith juggled, and the audience applauded.

"Where are my friends?" said the princess. "Perhaps they have forgotten my party." She began to cry. Nobody noticed.

Suddenly, the princess heard a familiar voice calling from far away. "Hellooo, little princess, hellooo."

The princess quickly dried her tears and ran to the window.

"They won't let me in!" cried the organ-grinder.

"Wait," shouted the princess, "don't go away. I will help you!"

The princess ran to the queen. "Mother!" she cried. "My friends are out there! Please invite them in."

"Will you be quiet!" shouted the queen. "Can't you see I am watching this beautiful perform-ance?"

"I thought this was *my* party," said the princess.

"The Philistine Palaver Poetry Players from Pelham," announced the major domo....

The princess found a rope and ran back to the window. She tied the rope to the window sill.

"Hurrah!" shouted the organ-grinder. "What a clever girl you are!" Then he and the monkey quickly climbed up the rope.

"Come, let's dance," whispered the princess.

The ballroom was very crowded and noisy now. The Sterling String Ensemble, The Kapusta Octet, The Noctambule Nonsense Dancers, The Juvenile Juggling Team of Pergolesi, Pergolesi, and Smith, and The Philistine Palaver Poetry Players were all performing at once.

"What a party! What a party!" cried the grandmothers and the aunts.

"Quite a spectacle," admitted the uncles.

"The grandest ever," said the queen to the king.

"The Fantastic Rope-Trick Fakir from Fandango!" announced the major domo.

"WHERE IS MY ROPE?" cried the Fakir from Fandango.

"WHERE IS THE PRINCESS?" shouted the king and queen.

When the princess was discovered dancing with a monkey and not sitting straight in her chair, a great uproar began.

The monkey became very frightened and ran through the crowd. He jumped on top of The Fakir, who fell on top of an Octet singer. She fell on top of one of the members of The String Ensemble, and broke his violin. The other singers stopped singing and began screaming, dancers began slipping and falling, Palaver Players were shouting....

"Do something," begged the queen. "What will my relatives say," she whimpered, and fainted.

"Catch that awful boy and his dirty animal!" raged the king.

"Run, run!" cried the princess.

But the organ-grinder and the monkey were soon caught and thrown into the dungeon.

"TOMORROW AT DAWN THEY WILL HANG!" commanded the king.

"DON'T HURT MY BEST FRIENDS!" cried the princess.

The queen was revived from her faint. "Ungrateful child," she screamed. "What a way to behave at such a nice party. Go to bed and stop sniveling!"

With bruised ankles and broken instruments, the performers left the palace. The grandmothers and uncles and aunts and cousins went to bed because the party was over.

The princess lay in bed and cried and cried. Then she stopped crying and began to think. She thought for a long time.

Late that night, the princess knew what she had to do. She got out of bed, put a dark cloak over her nightgown, and crept down to the dungeon, where the guards were snoring loudly. The princess stole the key and opened the doors for her friends.

"Take me away from here," she whispered to the organ-grinder.

The three friends took a horse from the stable and vanished into the night.

In the morning, the governesses found her bed empty and the princess gone.

The king and queen and everyone at court searched the palace from turret to dungeon. The king raged at the guards. The queen raged at the governesses.

But the princess, the boy, and the monkey could not be found.

The three friends fled to another country, far, far away.

Every morning, the princess woke with the sun and said to her friends, "Wake up, wake up. Here comes another lovely day to spend together!"

"Good morning," said the organ-grinder. "How pretty you look this morning."

The three friends kissed each other. They washed and dressed and ate wild strawberries for breakfast.

Then they traveled from village to town and danced and sang songs for all the people.

"What a sweet monkey!" cried the children.

"What a lovely girl," said the fathers.

"What a handsome boy," said the mothers.

People clapped and cheered and welcomed them everywhere.

When the sun set every evening, the princess, the organ-grinder, and the monkey were very tired and very happy.

"What a wonderful day we had today," said the princess.

"Yes, and tomorrow there will be another one," said the organ-grinder. "But now let's go to sleep."

"Good night, good night," they said. Then the three friends kissed one another and slept very well.

The End